Wasteland

Author's notes

Wasteland is a collection of short stage plays I wrote while studying Writing for Performance at Ruskin College, Oxford – from 2014 – 2016

Thank you – John Retallack, Helen Mosby, Namita Chakrabarty, Jan Thomas (Co-author *Boy*), Jessica Lee-Rice, Steven Holmes and Tony Thompson for all of your combined knowledge, guidance and support throughout my two years at Ruskin.

Stage directions are in (Italics)

A stroke (/) marks the point of interruption in overlapping dialogue.

Three dots (...) directly after a spoken word indicates a character is thinking about what to say next.

A horizontal line (–) at the end or mid spoken word indicates another character has cut them off.

A (Beat) signals a moment of pause or shift in a scene.

Punctuation is used to indicate delivery, not to conform to the rules of grammar.

Phonetic spelling is used for characters dialogue who speak with thick accents.

The plays are set out in sequence of when they were first written. Beginning with *Boys Don't Tell* and closing with *Hush Little Baby*. Therefore showing the development of my writing spanning two years.

Boys Don't Tell

Scene 1

Elvis Presley's Treat Me Nice plays just before lights go up and continues throughout the scene.

A man in his early forties stands over a woman of a similar age. She is clearly distressed, cowering on the floor of a living room decorated in Elvis memorabilia. She holds a framed picture of Elvis close to her chest as the man repeatedly beats her. He snatches the picture from her grasp and throws it at the wall, smashing it.

A boy aged 11 enters the stage holding a large knife in his hand. Neither man nor woman realise he is there. The boy stands with his back to the audience as he watches the attack unfold. The woman screams out and tries to protect herself by curling up into fetal position. The boy begins to sob and runs off stage, still holding the knife.

Music and lights fade.

Scene 2

A different boy, also 11, arrives home late to an angry mother of no particular age.

Mother: Where have you been? I've been worried sick Joshua!

Josh: Sorry mommy.

Mother: What time do you call this? I've told you already, I don't want you staying out after dark. You have no idea who's out there.

Josh: I know mommy. I'm sorry. Can I go upstairs now?

Mother: NO! You'll stay here. I'm not finished with you yet. Where have you been all night?

Silence.

Mother: Tell me Joshua... Have you been to those woods again?

Josh: Yeah ... but—

Mother: No buts mister. You know you're not allowed in the woods, don't you?

Josh: Yes mommy.

Mother: And you were with that Robbie boy too, wasn't you?

Josh: *(Head down)* Yeah.

Mother: I don't like you hanging around with that boy, Joshua. He's a bad influence on you. I've told you time and time again not to see him ... And I've told you not to go to the woods, yet you still disobey me!

Josh: I don't mommy and it—it was only this once.

Mother: That's not the point Joshua. If I tell you not to do something, then I expect you not to go and do it... *[Pause]* Right, you're grounded for a /week.

Josh: Ahhh but mom!

Mother: And you will stop seeing that Robbie boy too. Are we clear?

Josh: Yes mommy. Sorry mommy. Can I go to my room now, pleassse?

Mother: NO JOSH! You can go when I say you can. Look at you, you're filthy... Right, get upstairs and clean yourself up while I reheat your dinner. The dinner you failed to come home for earlier.

Lights fade.

Scene 3

Two boys, Robbie and Josh, both 11 walk through the woods as the evening sun breaks through the trees.

Robbie: He's lucky I neva killed him.

Josh: Could you of?

Robbie: Err yeah – course I cudda. I've got a knife ya know.

Josh: Yeah? Sick! Let's see?

Robbie: It's a proppa one an' everyfink. Like Rambo's! My big bro gave it me.

Josh: Wow... It's really big. And heavy!

Robbie: Yeah and sharp. You wanna watch it. An' if ya tell anyone I've got it, I'll smash ya face in, oright?

Josh: Yeah course, I wudent say nufink. I swear down, Robbie.

Robbie: Good.

Josh: So why didn't ya stick ya dad then? I wudda, if my dad was batterin' me mom.

Robbie: Nah, he ent werf it. I left him to it. But I had to get out that place. My mom's a full on loon. She does me ed'in wiv all that Elvis shit in the house. Photos of him everywhere and not onea me. An all she ev'a does is play his shitty music as she wipes the picture frames... No wonda me old man hits her... I ent goin' back home now though. That's it. I'm finally free. I can do what I want, when I want. I don't need parents ... a loon and a drunk *(laughs)* who needs that shit. Fuck 'em!

Josh: What ya gonna do then?

Robbie: Live he'a.

Josh: Innn theee wooods?

Robbie: Yeah course. I've got me knife to hunt wiv ... An' I can build a house in the trees an everyfink.

Josh: What about ya PlayStation ... and TV?

Robbie: I don't need 'em Josh.

Josh: I swear, I couldn't live wivout me PlayStation.

Robbie: Yeah but I'm olda than ya, ent I?

Josh: Only by a month.

Robbie: Yeah an what? That makes me olda and betta so there. And me big bro's taught me stuff too. He showed me how ya kill someone wiv one punch, crushin' their nose into their brainsss! Watch, I'll show ya. Lean ya head back like this *[Robbie positions Joshes' head]* and then I punch ya like this. BAM straight in the nose, shovin' it up into ya brain. It'll kill ya instantly, swear down. And I can kill anyone wiv this move so don't mess wiv me or I'll use it on you, oright?

Josh: Ahhh that's so cool.

Robbie: Did ya he'a about the crazy old geeza who lives he'a? Like, he's only got one arm and everyfink.

Josh: What? Na there ent.

Robbie: There is. I swear on me mom's life.

Josh: Ya shouldn't do that.

Robbie: What?

Josh: Swear on ya mom's life. That's harsh.

Robbie: Naa, what ya on about. It's oright coz I ent lyin', so there. An' anyway, I don't give a shit about me mom. Moms are for pussies like you.

Robbie laughs in Joshes face.

Josh: No I ent. Shut up.

Robbie: Yeah ya are. Little Josh scared of his mommy.

Josh: What ya on about? I'm not.

Robbie: Prove it then. Live wiv me in the woods. We can survive out he'a. I know stuff. It's easy to survive. We can live off the land … and hunt shit. I'm sure there's deer or sumink like that round he'a … and we can build a tree house like in Robin Hood. C'mon it'll be—

Josh: I ent sure Robbie. I need to be back for me dinna soon. Me mom'll be fumin' if I'm late.

Robbie: Don't be a pussy. Ya don't need ya mom. Parents are cock munchin' shits. Ya dad thought that about ya mom, remember?

Silence.

Robbie: Coz my dad shagged your mom … Remember?

Josh: Shut up Robbie! Stop sayin' that shit. He neva!

Robbie: Yeah, well it's true. Ya know that's why ya dad ran away, don't ya? That's why ya mom won't tell ya why he left … My old man told me everyfink. He said ya dad couldn't handle the fort of ya mom shaggin' my old man. *(Laughs)* To be honest, I bet my dad's still shaggin' her. Like, fink about it. My mom's a full on nut job, who only cares about Elvis fuckin' Presley, so why's the old man gonna wanna do her when your mom's only a few doors down. *(Laughs again)* An' she loves it coz my dad's a real man.

Josh: Shut the fuck up! You're a prick Robbie.

Robbie: Oright, chill out dick'ed. I'm only sayin' what happened.

Josh: Yeah well ya dad's a wanka for what he did.

Robbie punches Josh in the gut, knocking him down.

Robbie: Ya don't get to say shit about my old man, oright?

Silence.

Robbie: C'mon get up. *(Robbie puts his hand out)* I'll help ya up... You ev'a felt a girls tits?

Silence.

Robbie: Yeah fort not ... Ya gay or sumink?

Josh: NO!

Robbie: *(Laughs)* Bet you are. You're gay.

Josh: Shut up! Av you ev'a? Ha, bet you ent.

Robbie: Yeah course I av. I'm always feelin' bird's tits. The girls love it. I've shagged 'em an everyfink.

Josh: Ahh, av ya? I wish I could shag a girl. What's it like?

Robbie: Yeah, ya will one day. And ya gotta snog 'em before ya shag 'em Josh. You ev'a tonged a girl?

Josh: Nah. What's it like?

Robbie: It's slimy an' messy. Lucy Young snogs like a proppa fish.

Josh: When did ya snog her?

Robbie: The other day. Round the back of the P.E block. She let me grab her tits n'all.

Josh: She's proppa fit as well.

Robbie: Err... yeah course she is, but she can't snog for shit.

Josh: Did ya shag her?

Robbie: Nah, not after I tonged her. I almost puked in her gob.

Both boys laugh.

Josh: So who av ya shagged?

Robbie: No one you'd know.

Josh: What's it like? I wanna know!

Robbie: Like, don't get a bonner or any fink. Like, it's good n'all but—

Josh: What?

Robbie: Well, it's not as good as... like say... Alton Towers or Go-kartin' or sumink fun like that. But it's oright like.

Josh: Urrghh, that's shit. Adults make out like it's the best. Girls do me ed'in anyway.

Robbie: Yeah fuck 'em. I'm bored. C'mon let's do sumink fun... What's that ov'a there? C'mon...

The boys come across an old fire, with a few empty beer crates and a log positioned around the ashes. There is a makeshift rope-swing attached to the tree.

Lights fade.

Scene 4

Josh is sat at the dinner table eating while his mother is sat opposite him.

Josh: Mom?

Mother: Yes Josh?

Josh: Why did dad leave?

Mother: You know why, Josh.

Josh: No, why did he really leave?

Mother: I've already told you why. Things just weren't working between us... You know this already Josh... *(Pause)* I know it hasn't been long and it's still going to take time to come to terms with. But you're still going to see your father. He's not going anywhere, he's just moved out.

Josh: You're lyin'.

Mother: What? No I'm not, Josh. Where's this come from all of a sudden?

Josh: You shagged Robbie's dad, didn't ya?

Mother: I beg your pardon young man. What did you just say?

Josh: You heard me. Ya shagged him, didn't ya?

Mother: How dare you talk to me like that, Joshua. And where the hell did you learn language like that?

Josh: Stop lyin' mom. That's why dad left, wasn't it? I hate you!

Mother: Stop lying...? *(Pause)* What are you talking about? Of course I didn't do anything with Robbie's father. I... I can't even believe I'm having this conversation with you. Where did you hear such a ridiculous thing like that...? Oh, wait, I know. It's that Robbie, isn't it?

Silence.

Mother: He's the one filling your head with this rubbish. Look Joshua, I DID NOT cheat on your father with anybody, and certainly not with Robbie's father.

Josh: Well Robbie's dad told Robbie you did.

Mother: Did he now?

Josh: YEAH.

Mother: Or did Robbie just make it up for a stupid, childish joke? Look Joshua. You shouldn't believe everything Robbie tells you. He's a liar, and he's going to be in big trouble tomorrow when I go to see his father to sort out this ludicrous rumour he's made up.

A knock on the front door interrupts Josh and his mother. The mother gets up and goes to answer. Its Robbie's father, Frank. Josh runs upstairs and hides under his bed.

Frank: Alright love? Sorry to be a bother but is my lad here?

Mother: Err... no Frank, sorry. I thought he was with you?

Frank: Oh right … alright then *(Frank goes to leave but stops)* but, I'm confused now, coz I thought he was here. It's getting on for eleven now and I haven't seen the little bugger since he done a runner this morning. I'm getting a bit concerned. It's not like our lad to miss his grub.

Mother: Well Josh has been back for about an hour now and I just presumed Robbie had gone straight home … Hold on Frank, let me ask Josh.

Joshes mother stands at the foot of the stairs and shouts up to Josh, who is still hiding under his bed.

Mother: Josh… *(Silence)* Joshua… do you know where Robbie is? His father's at the door.

Silence.

Mother: Ugh. I really do wonder what's going on inside that boys head sometimes. He's been acting odd ever since he got in. Oh and Frank. *(Mother whispers)* I know this is bound to sound ridiculous to you too, but I need to ask… Did you make anything up about the two of us having an affair?

Frank: Sorry love, you what?

Mother: I'm sorry for asking that. But I only ask because Josh has just had this outburst and he's pretty adamant that you've told Robbie that the two of us had an affair, and that was the reason his father left.

Frank: What? No, no, of course I didn't. That's a ridiculous thing to say. Why the hell would I say that?

Mother: I know. And that's exactly what I thought. I knew it. Your Robbie's made this up.

Frank: But why would he?

Mother: I'm not sure, Frank. You and I both know kids can do some strange things, sometimes.

Frank: Yep that's true. And it does sound like something that little shit would say. Well I tell you what, I'll be having some serious words with that lad when I get my hands on him. Bloody idiots probably out robbing some old lady as we speak.

Mother: *(Puckered eyebrows)* Well okay, Frank. I'm glad we got to the bottom of that. Let me go up and have a word with him and if I find anything out about Robbie I'll pop round and let you know, alright?

Frank: Yep, alright then love. Thanks for your help.

Mother: No problem.

Mother shuts the door and goes upstairs to find Josh. His legs are sticking out from under his bed.

Mother: What are you doing under there mister?

Silence.

Mother: Hey, I'm talking to you. C'mon out now...

Silent, Josh stays under the bed.

Mother: I'm not in the mood to play games, Joshua. Why are you acting like this, huh? And where's Robbie? Where did he go after you FINALY came home?

Josh: I don't wonna.

Mother: You don't want to what?

Josh: Talk … I ent sayin' nufink… *(Long pause)* Did you really not cheat on dad wiv Robbie's dad?

Mother: *(Softer voice)* Of course I didn't, Josh. Now stop this and come out from under there. And, do you know where Robbie is?

Josh: He said he's gone to live in the woods for ev'a.

Josh starts weeping under the bed.

Mother: What's wrong, Josh?

Josh: Mommy, I fink I've done a bad fing.

Lights fade.

Scene 5

Both boys are at the abandoned camp as dusk sets in.

Robbie: This is so cool. Let's do the bit in Robin Hood where they hang the prisoners, yeah?

Josh: Yeah oright.

Robbie: You get on the log an' tie the rope around ya neck an' then I'll be Robin Hood an' I'll come an' save ya.

Josh: Why do you get to be Robin Hood?

Robbie: Coz my names Robbie… Robin. Same name enit?

Josh: Not really.

Robbie: Yeah it is. I'm Robin oright?

Josh: That ent fair. Let's do rock paper scissors for it?

Robbie: Nah! My names Robbie so I should be Robin Hood.

Josh: Well I ent playin' then.

Robbie: Don't be a dick'ed Josh.

Josh: I wanna be Robin Hood.

Robbie: Well ya can't be him.

Josh: Fine, I'm goin' home then.

Josh walks away.

Robbie: Oi wait dick'ed. Ya can be such a div sometimes, ya know that? Oright rock paper scissors then. Best outa three, oright?

The boys play the game three times, Robbie loses twice.

Robbie: That ent fair. YOU CHEATED!

Josh: No I neva!

Robbie: Best outa five?

Josh: Na, I'm Robin Hood.

Robbie: This is a fuckin joke...

Josh: I need a sword. Give me ya knife Robbie?

Robbie gives Josh his knife and then gets on one of the crates and ties the rope around his neck.

Robbie: Josh, ride in on ya horse then an' save me.

Josh: Oright.

Josh pretends to ride over to Robbie on an imaginary horse. He stops and tries to pull the crate from under Robbie's feet. Robbie panics, struggling to stay perched on the crate. Robbie puts the crate back and Robbie unties himself, jumps off the crate and punches Josh, knocking him down.

Robbie: What the fuck did ya do that for, dick'ed?

Josh: Shit, sorry Robbie. It was just a joke. That's all.

Robbie: You're a fuckin' dick'ed Josh. Go back home where ya belong and be a mommy's boy. Me dad'll be round late'a to tuck you in.

Robbie laughs.

Josh: Shut it Robbie.

Robbie: Err… na your oright fanks. My dad's gonna love layin' into ya mom tonight. *(Laughs)* You're a faggot just like ya dad. That's why he left too, ya know? He's proppa gay an' shit.

Josh: Shut the fuck up ya prick. You're lyin'!

Robbie: Na I ent. Now fuck off back to mommy.

Robbie turns and walks away. In a fit of rage, Josh gets to his feet and picks up the knife. He thrusts it into Robbie's back. Robbie drops to his knees and keels over dead.

Lights fade.

Scene 6

The mother, horrified and speechless by what Josh has just told her, runs over to the phone. Josh follows, crying.

Josh: Mommy. I neva meant it. I just wanted him to shut up, that's all... I didn't want him to die. I promise.

Mother: I can't even believe my ears. WHAT HAVE YOU DONE?!

The mother picks up the phone and starts to dial. Josh stands in front of her sobbing. She looks at him and then looks at her car keys. She places the phone on the side, grabs the keys and takes Joshes hand. They walk out the front door shutting it behind them.

End

Boy

*A woman stands on one side of the stage. She is thin,
around forty and has short hair. She smiles at the
audience but her stance is tense.*

*The other side of the stage a boy. He looks angry,
resentful, has attitude in the way he stands and the way
he looks at the audience.*

WOMAN
He was such a sweet little boy, an angel.

LUCAS
He brought it on himself. I ent takin' all the blame.

WOMAN
He had the whole package, blond curls, big blue eyes and
he adored his mummy.

LUCAS
I grew up with Randel. We were like best mates as kids.
Even though he was a scrawny fucker, with funny, curly
blonde hair.
(Pause)
And he was a bit too smart for me n'all, but he made me
laugh. I was always creasin' at him.

WOMAN
His father was hopeless of course, they never really
bonded.

LUCAS
It weren't my fault… Ya know, the bullyin' an' stuff. There
were others involved too.

WOMAN
I'd even say he was jealous. Isn't that a terrible thing for a father to be jealous of his own son? Anyway, I said to Randel we're better off without him. I cried a bit, well you do don't you even if it's for the best? Randel just kissed my face over and over.

LUCAS
It's just the way it is at school. Its dog eat dog. You join in or you get bullied yourself. Like, what was I meant to do?

WOMAN
He was four when Chris left.

LUCAS
He used to come round mine and we'd play football in my garden. He made me crease cos he was so shit at football. I liked playin' him cos I'm bigger than him, so I could always push him off the ball and I was always able to win.

WOMAN
(Sighs) Of course they have to grow up and I decided there and then... You hear so much nonsense about single mothers. But of course they're talking about those council house types. You'd see them outside the school, smoking. I told Randel smoking was stupid and if I ever caught even a whiff on him, I'd kill him.

LUCAS
I used to steal my old man's smokes when he fell asleep watchin' the weekly scores. I'd try an' get Randel to smoke them with me but he would never touch 'em. He always had this really scared look on his face. Like, he was even brickin' it in case the smell got on his clothes.

WOMAN
Anyway where was I? Oh yes, I decided Randel was going to be a great success. I could see he was above average intelligence and he did so well at primary. Nice little school.

LUCAS
He would always stare at my Airs Maxes. 'I'm gonna get some of them soon,' he'd say, while he messed with his manky Velcro strap school shoes. He wore them all the time, it was embarrassing being around him sometimes.

WOMAN
I took a job closer to home. It meant a bit less money but Randel had never been one of those kids who wanted all the latest stuff, Nike trainers and all that rubbish. Sweatshop labour I told him, all those poor, children in some hot country working fifteen hours a day for a dollar just so Nike can make money selling shoes to gullible kids. He said it was all right, he didn't need them.

LUCAS
To be honest, I did rip it out of him for wearin' his school shoes all the time. And that stupid big guitar thing he always carried round on his back got me in stitches an' all. But I was only havin' a laugh. I never used to hit him or anything.

WOMAN
I did splash out on the cello though. I read somewhere that learning an instrument helps cognitive development. He loved his cello. That's why I can't understand...

LUCAS

Everything was all right until I got picked for school's football team last year. That was when I met Sara. She was the fittest girl at school and every boy wanted to get with her. She was always at the matches, cheering us on. I started chillin' with her cos she was mates with some of the lads from the team. An' before I knew it we were together. We were only seein' each other at first but after a few weeks we were officially boyfriend and girlfriend.

I really liked Sara, I was properly in love with her. I popped my cherry with her an everything! She made me crease so much. We used to do everything together and she was always at my matches cheerin' me on. She made me feel like I was worth something, ya know? I'm kinda glad she's gone now.

WOMAN

There was real anger in it, that's what hurt the most. You could see he'd smashed it, stamped on it, torn it to pieces.
(Pause)
I blame those kids, that one most of course. They made him hate his cello. They made him hate me.

LUCAS

I was chillin' with Sara against the P.E block wall when Randel walked past. He was comin' from his music class and he had that huge fuckin thing on his back, like usual. He spotted me chillin' and tried to come over and speak to me.

WOMAN

I just don't understand why he did it.

LUCAS
Alright, I said. Then Sara nudged me and was like: 'what you doin' talkin' to him for? Look at him, he's a fuckin' mong!'

She was so nice, I didn't wanna disagree with her or she might of dumped me.

'Fuck off, Ya fuckin' mong!' I shouted, givin' him my hardest look. He looked confused at first and tried to say something else but I stopped him by pushin' myself off the wall and getting up in his face. He started shakin' I yanked his guitar thing off his back and threw it on the concrete.

WOMAN
He changed. From a bright, sunny little boy he turned into this horrible, sullen thing. He liked to sleep in my bed. Then one day he said he was a big boy now and wanted to sleep in his own bed. He hardly spoke a word when he got home from school. Went straight to his room. Said he had homework. Well I respected that, of course, but I wished he'd do it downstairs. I said I could help but he said they were supposed to do it themselves.

LUCAS
We saw him again the week after. He was carrying' that thing on his back like it was a fuckin' Jesus cross or something. His hair was funny an' all. We started to shout 'Goldielocks' for a laugh.

'Oi Goldielocks, ya fuckin' pussy, come here!'

WOMAN
I said to him, what part of 'help' don't you understand?
I'm not going to do it for you. I expect other mums do, not
the ones from the council estate of course. But that
would explain why he started slipping down the league
table. I blame the school, I told his teacher he was always
top of the class at his old school, so how could she explain
that?

LUCAS
It was only small things like the hair an' stuff, but – but
Sara used to always take it too far. It wasn't my fault!

WOMAN
She brushed me off, said something about Randel's social
skills. Bloody cheek, he's always been such a polite boy. I
went to Ofsted. I have to say they responded very well.
They sent an inspector, talked to all the teachers, and
some of the students, and got Randel extra Maths and
English lessons.

LUCAS
'Oi Goldielocks! Come here!'

Sara shouted to him while he was crossin' the school field.
For the past few days a few of us got interviewed by some
people in suits, I didn't really pay much attention to them
to be honest, but Sara wasn't happy with it.

'Why we getting into shit cos of your mom?'

Randel didn't say much. He tried to walk away but Sara
grabbed his shirt and yanked him back, ripping it some.

WOMAN

I mean I'm not one of those helicopter mums, God forbid, but you have to stand up for your kids don't you? Schools these days don't care about the clever children. It's all dyslexia and special learning needs. I agree with that of course but they seem to forget that when a child is especially bright they have special needs too. They need to be challenged, stimulated. That school was no good for Randel, I see that now.

LUCAS

She yanked his shirt harder to make it rip more. Then she brought up a big greeny and gobbed in his face. Randel was wearin' a scarf too and Sara started to strangle him with it, while I kept lookout. He was chockin' a lot and Sara was really gettin' into it. Just before I thought he was gonna die she stopped it. His eyes had gone all red and he was panickin'. She took his scarf from him and we started to walk away. Randel got up and ran over to us.
'Give it back...' he shouted.
'Please give it back, please.'
'Give it back or my mom will kill me!'

We both laughed and Sara said
'He ah then, fetch.'

She threw it in a muddy puddle and Randel ran over to get it out.

WOMAN

We used to have these lovely Saturdays. After his cello practice, I'd make his favourite, Alphabeti Spaghetti and mashed banana with chocolate sauce and we'd sit and chat. He's such a bright boy I had to remind myself sometimes he was only a boy. I think I'm a good mother.

LUCAS
After we had been playin' football at the park Randel
invited me to his for tea. It was weird cos he'd never
asked me before.

WOMAN
Then one Saturday that boy was round. I made Randel's
special lunch and served it up to them. The boy sniggered
and Randel looked at the plates like they were... well. And
he said it wasn't his favourite anymore. His voice was so
nasty. I was furious.
(Laughs nervously)
I must admit I lost it a bit then.

LUCAS
His mum made us Alphabeti Spaghetti and some dodgy,
manky lookin' desert... Like, how old did she think we
was?
Anyway, I could tell Randel was embarrassed cos of what
he said.

'Mum it's not my favourite anymore. I'm 14 now.'

That was it then. His mom went into fuckin' mental retard
mode. She proppa lost her shit.

'Yes it is Randel!' She snapped.

'Don't try and show off in front of him.'

She pointed at me and gave me a stare that made me shit
it. We were starvin' and I would of still eaten the food but

the bitch wiped it all into the bin.

'If you boys want it, then you'll have to eat from the bin, because I'm not cooking again for you ungrateful sods.'

I didn't eat until I got home that night. I was that starvin' I ate a whole pack of Wagon Wheels to myself. I felt sorry for Randel as I scoffed 'em cos I don't think he got anything to eat again that night.

Randel never stuck up for himself normally and he proppa impressed me when he stood up for himself over the food. Even though it backfired on him, that was something he didn't do enough. But anyway, Randel's house weren't a nice place to chill and I never went back after that night.

WOMAN
Never saw the boy after that. I just assumed they'd had a falling out, they do at that age. I never realised... He should have told me... I could have nipped it in the bud then and there.

LUCAS
It was just after that I got picked for the football team.

WOMAN
(She becomes more animated, angry.)
He asked for Nikes. Well I said, I thought we'd agreed about that. He just muttered something about all the other kids and I said, 'if all the other kids jumped off a cliff would you jump too?' I think I got my point across, he didn't ask again.

LUCAS
I wish he hadn't of done what he did. Well no, I wish I
hadn't of pushed him to the point of doin' what he did. I
just hope he's okay! I'm going to make it up to him when
he's better. Teach him how to properly play football and
we'll hangout again. Well I hope he'll want to anyway.

WOMAN
(Her anger is growing. She begins to make chopping
motions with her hands as she speaks)
It's all that boys fault, that...
(Spits out the next word)
That Lucas. If I could get my hands on him.

LUCAS
Randel come running over to us with his muddy scarf.

'Look at it now, you've ruined it. My mom's going to kill
me if she sees it like this.'

Sara just laughed in his face.

'Aw, poor Randel, scared of his mummy over a fuckin'
scarf.'

She pushed her forehead into his face.

'Fuckin' do one Goldielocks.' I said, hoping he would leave
it. But he didn't.
(Pause)
Sara kicked him between his legs and Randel fell down.
She kicked him again while he was down. She pushed his
face into the muddy puddle. I was worried he was going
to drown.

'Sara, come on, Stop it. You're gonna kill him.' She stopped pushin' down on his head and let him breathe.

I told her we should leave before we got caught by a teacher. She said she just wanted to whisper something in his ear first.
(Pause)
She crouched down to his ear and whispered something but I couldn't hear what she said and when she finished she took a proppa hard bite to his ear, making it bleed.
(Pause)
And that was it, he got up, cryin' his eyes out. I watched him run off. Then the hospital called and now I'm here, waitin.'

WOMAN
Last Christmas it was I got him the scarf. We'd seen one of the musicians wearing one like it at the jazz club. We used to go together Sunday afternoons. He said he liked it so I spent a whole day searching the web to find one exactly the same. He loved it at first. But then... Finding him like that. It's the worst thing a mother can see.

She looks up as if someone has come into the room.

Is he awake? The nurses wouldn't tell me anything.
(Beat)
What do you mean?
(Beat)
What kind of man are you to tell a mother something like that? It isn't true.
(Beat, then she emits a primal scream)
Noooooooooooo!

She begins to hit with her fists at the unseen doctor, sobbing and screaming all the time. Then she freezes, looks at her hands and lowers them. She becomes very still, stands straight.

I want to see him.
(Beat)
I don't care. I want to see him. Now. He's next door isn't he? I know he is. I saw him earlier.

The woman struggles with the unseen doctor. She gets free and steps into Lucas's space on stage. She is confronting him in the room next door. He has his head hung low, sobbing. He drops to his knees at her feet. The Woman looks down at his bent head.

WOMAN
You are nothing, less than nothing. He was worth ten of you. You'll never amount to anything, you'll have a wasted, useless life and you'll die alone.

She spits on his head, kicks him away and leaves. Lucas stays on the floor sobbing, composes himself and then gets up.

LUCAS
My friend is dead. He took his own life because of me.
(Pause)
How can I live with that? I can't believe he's gone. For good. It doesn't feel true. I keep thinking I'll wake up and everything will be back to normal and I'll get to see him again.
I really thought he'd be okay I was gonna make it up to him. I was gonna be his mate again. This time though I

was gonna be a real mate.

(Pause)

I wish I could turn back... change things. I really do! But –
but it's not that– He's dead.

End

Go

GO: He makes me wish my senses would shut down for good,

With his stale, panting breath, making me heave.

His bristles grating against my skin, leaving me red-raw.

His sweaty, fat fucking gut sticking to my tummy.

With no care in the world he pushes his unwashed penis in far too hard,

Forcing my period to come on premature.

Every inch of my being is repulsed by this man

I can't take anymore.

'STOP!'

'Please *stop*.'

I'm ignored.

So I try and push him off with my hands but he's too strong.

He delivers an overwhelming blow to my face.

I can't open my right eye.

I can't even feel it.

I'm scared I might be blind.

I feel so sleepy it makes me stop struggling.

It's happening again.

I'm being raped.

Beat.

He finishes and pulls out

'I ain't payin' full to fuck a ragdoll.' He screams, showering my face in a mist of drool.

He pulls up his jeans, takes out a battered ten pound note and throws it at the floor.

I'm just glad it's over.

Beat.

I thought he was going to be one of the good ones. But you never know who you're going to get until it's too late.

We call them the good punters.

The ones who don't hit us. They are normally gentle, even charming at times… But apart from them not getting that primeval urge to rupture a blood vessel in my eye or fracture a cheekbone, there's nothing *good* about the good punters.

They are the ones who ask how my days been… after they've fucked me, of course. It's always after. Their too desperate to bust their fucking nut to do anything before. But once business is seen to they start with the questions.

They asks how I got the bands of purple bruising around my wrists. Or how the shiner teasing its way through my foundation was caused. They always ask the same fucking questions.

'Is someone hurting you?'

'Are you going to be okay?'

'What can I do to help?'

Trying their best to sound concerned as they run that soul destroying hand though my hair, still infatuated by what they just did to me.

They think you're their fucking girlfriend sat in that car.

Trying to get more than they've paid for.

Running fingers across my exposed torso. Sending tremors through me with their corrosive touch.

They actually think it's okay. Like their money gives them that fucking right.

Beat.

I don't want to be cuddled or touched by the creep who just violated my most intimate locations.

Expecting me to laugh with them as they crack their pathetic dad jokes... Because that's what most of them are.

Isn't it?

Dads.

Fathers to children who have no idea about their daddy's sordid secret life.

They are meant to be our protectors, not abusers!

Beat.

Most of the cars I get in are family cars. Sometimes still with rattles or dummies on the backseats. Or them baby-on-board stickers in the back windows.

Only the other night, one of the good punters literally had his fucking baby on board when he pulled up. I didn't realise until I was on top. Just trying to get the job done quick as so I could get paid and get out.

I looked up and saw this *beautiful* little baby girl in front of me. The poor thing couldn't have been more than six months old.

It made me sick.

I shut my eyes and looked away, trying to blank out her presence. Wishing it over quicker than before.

Thank God she was fast asleep. All wrapped up in her pink car seat.

Beat.

And yes. I get hurt every fucking day.

I get punched, kicked, head-butted. Normally for no reason.

I get raped, gobbed on. My body used as an ashtray. I've even been pissed on. You name it.

All because I'm classed as a skank. The lowest of the low who shouldn't expect any better.

People can be so cruel when they see you as nothing more than shit on their shoe.

Beat.

But it's not always physical.

This is what the good punters still don't get. They wants to fuck me and know my darkest, deepest feelings. Feelings I can't even begin to process. So why the fuck would I tell them?

They're so fucking stupid. Wrapped up in their pathetic self-centered lives that they fail to see the irony in their questions.

They are the ones harming me *too*.

They are the ones who keep me clocking in and clocking out, night after night.

And these men are your neighbors, husbands ... fathers ... brothers.

I might even be standing in front of some right now.

Beat.

I always wonder about the men that pay for my body. Good or bad... How can they justify their actions?

How do they lie to themselves...? Thinking it's alright when it's the furthest thing from alright.

Like nothing's happened when only hours or even minutes before they paid for a vulnerable girl's body.

Girls sometimes younger than their own daughters.

Underage girls touched by men who would never normally dream of molesting a child. But because a fourteen year-old girl stands on the same street as us, promoting herself like we do. Smiling, trying her hardest to look like she wants it, when all she really wants is to be loved and looked after. Suddenly it's okay?

Maybe it's just sheer ignorance. Or maybe they know exactly what they pull up for. I don't know.

All I know is none of us would be doing this if we had the choice.

It's a necessity. It's the only way we know how to survive.

Beat.

But there comes a time, like tonight when what you do to stay alive begins to make you feel like you're already dead. And then I just think, what's the point?

Beat.

I'm finishing early tonight.

The nights you get raped are often early finishes. Unless you have a debt to pay off or a drug habit to feed. Then you have no choice but to stay out.

Beat.

As I walk home I contemplate taking my life.

No more pain. No nothing. Just sleep.

I think about it a lot, but I never actually do it.

I don't want to die. It's just it seems like it would be easier sometimes, that's all.

I walk into an off-license and walk out with a litre bottle of vodka

Beat.

I'm not far from mine when a car pulls up and the window drops down. I don't stop. I don't even look to see who's interested. I just want to get home and sleep.

'Excuse me.'

I stop walking.

I've stopped because it's not a man's voice calling from the car.

She tells me her names Vicky. She's a caseworker with a charity called Beyond the Streets.

'I'm Go.'

'Nice to meet you, Go.'

Vicky offers me a hot coffee from her flask. And a cheese and pickle sandwich.

It feels good to get a hot drink and some food down me.

She offers to drive me to the hospital so they can fix my eye but I turn her down. No point. I just want to go home and sleep.

Vicky hands me a pack of condoms and a pamphlet.

She tells me Beyond the Streets can help.

'It's a prostitution recovery centre that focuses on recovery from trauma and adversity.'

She tries to reassure me.

'We're committed to helping girls in your position, Go. Come to the shelter first thing tomorrow and I'll personally get you signed up, yeah? There's more to life than working these streets, my love.'

She gives me a hug goodbye and heads back into the city center to give out more condoms and pamphlets.

She exits the stage.

End

Hush Little Baby

Cast of characters

All characters aged seventeen
Lina
Connor
Birdie
Matty

Setting

A rundown council estate somewhere in Birmingham. The location only ever referred to as *Town*.

Glossary

Bine is slang for cigarette.
Bluey is five pounds
Spice is a legal high, readily available from behind the counter. It is affordable and smoked like cannabis but its high is similar to heroin and is extremely addictive.

One

Lina

Cradles a crying baby – only weeks old.

Hush, little baby, don't say a word.
Papa's gonna buy you a mockingbird

And if that mockingbird won't sing,
Papa's gonna buy you a diamond ring –

Baby stops crying.

I don't like people
I don't like depending on them
Because people leave
I suppose, it's human nature
People leave
They move on
Runaway
Die

So you only really have yourself

But people can be addictive
So addictive
They are the best kind of drug with the best kind of high
And it's too easy to become hooked
Dependent on them
To crave their company

Their Love

And that's dangerous
Because everything's fucked from that point
The point you know you can't be without them
So then you're just left waiting for it
The day you come home and find them gone
No explanation
Just gone
Or they die
But it's sometimes better that way
Because at least you know they didn't leave because of
you

To survive you have to learn how to be alone
By yourself
Not depending on anyone else to keep all your pieces
together
You have to

And I do
I want to survive
I try
Everyday
But it's hard
Loneliness
It gets in 'n spreads
Burrowing in deep to your bones where it stays
Like a disease
Eating away at your vital organs
You can be surrounded by hundreds or even thousands of
people

But still have that sickening barren block inside
consuming you
And that's not there when you're with someone positive
Who wants to spend time with you
Care for you
Love you
So you want to be around them all the time
Day and night
Because they seem to fix everything
They keep the loneliness at bay.

Until they leave
Then where does that leave you?

Baby starts crying.
Lights fade.

Two

Lina

I met a boy today
His name's Connor
I've never known a Connor before
He's different
Nice
Cute
A bit shy
Ginger

Never gone for a ginger lad before
Never done anything with a ginger to be fair
I normally go for tall lads with dark hair
But Connor's still good-looking though
And he's tall
His hair's cut really short so you can't even tell he's ginger
He looks more blonde from a distance

I can tell he's not like other boys
He's not loud 'n in your face
Most boys are like wolves
Rabid pack animals who just wanna fuck
Obsessed with threesomes 'n anal
Like they think everything's fuckin porn

Connors's more like
A fox
A cute red fox
It's his eyes
Their soft, gentle eyes
They remind me of Maltesers

You can tell a lot from someone's eyes
You get vibes
I think it's something to do with their colours
Their intensity, you know?
I don't like cold eyes
The kind that seem to go straight through you
Connor's are warm
Big brown ones
Like milk chocolate Maltesers, sprinkled in tiny specs of
dark chocolate

His eyes were the first thing I noticed
He was already looking at me
But I couldn't tell if he was smiling or about to sneeze
I think he was smiling though
But he looked away so fast
So I moved and sat next to him
We talked
He was actually interested in me
Asking me where I'm from 'n stuff
Beat.
I've invited him to mine tonight
I don't know what come over me
I never invite people round
But he makes me smile when I think of him
I haven't stopped smiling all day
And that's rare

I've just been to get my hair done
Do you like it?
I really like it
I've never bothered getting it done before
It cost a bomb
But
I want to impress him

I hope he likes it

Baby starts crying.
Lights fade.

Three

Town streets – Birdie, Matty and Connor stand on the street corner.

Matty. There's fuck all to do in this town. It duz my fuckin 'eadin'.

Birdie. Coz it's a fuckin shit'ole bruv. What you expect?

Matty. Fuckin chillin' out 'ear like some fuckin bag'eads. Its jokes man.

Birdie. We just gotta start earnin' 'n well be outa 'ear man.

How longs ya man gonna be?

Matty. He said ten minutes, like forty fuckin minutes ago.

Birdie. Paki minutes though ennit bruv. Gonna be waitin' time.

Matty. This is wank bruv. He best 'urry the fuck up man. I can't fuckin stand this cold.

Birdie. What you ask for?

Matty. Two G's.

Birdie. Two fuckin G's?

Matty. Yeah?

Birdie. An 'ow we meant to earn wiv two fuckin G's?
Fuck sake Matty.

Matty. Detergent dick'ead. Two grams becomes five.

Birdie. Yeah I fuckin know that, we need more though.
They'll clock on if we cut the shit too much.

Matty. *Tuts.* Chill bruv.
What can we do?
We got no more doe.

Birdie. *To Connor.* 'Ow much you got?

Connor. Err... fifty pounds... But I –

Birdie. Buzzin'. Give it Matty.

Connor. Nah, I can't.

Birdie. What you on about?
You wanna make some doe, ennit?

Connor. Yeah... but... it's my –

Birdie. What?

Connor. It's me birfdee money.
It's for new trainers.

Matty. So, who gives a fuck?

Connor. It's just I need it... My mum'll screw if I don't 'av
new trainers.

Matty. FUCK 'ER!
It's your money.
You can do what ya want wiv it, ennit?

Birdie. Once we sort this little earner out, you'll be able to
buy two pairs a trainers.
To Matty. Or just one decent pair. Aaa ha.
You want in, ennit?
C'mon.

Connor. Yeah but... I can't though Birdie, sorry man.
Matty. Fuck sake Connor. Stop bein' a little pussy boy.

Birdie. Give Matty the money Connor.

Connor. But I – I –

Matty. I – I – I DERRRRR! Fuckin retard. Get it out.

Birdie. Leave it for a sec Matty.
Ignore 'im Connor.
Look. If you give us that fifty we'll give you hundred back.

Yeah?
Sounds good, ennit?

Connor. I really wanna help ya Birdie. You know I do. I really like ya... but –

Birdie. Well help me then, ennit.
C'mon. You're the man, ent ya?
We'll all be equal partners.
Split it wiv ya fifty-fifty between the three of us.

Yeah?

Connor. When will I get the hundred?

Birdie. Like straight away. Pretty much.

Connor. I'm not sure Birdie... I really need this money man. I'm really sorry.

Matty. HE'S HERE!

Birdie. Connor the money.

Connor. Guys I –

Matty. QUICK! Fuck sake. I can't leave 'im waitin'.

Birdie. CONNOR!

Matty. C'MON! Fuckin give it now ya prick before I fuckin deck ya.

Connor hands the money to Matty.
Lights fade.

Four

Town streets.

Matty. Don't tell 'er that shit, you fuckin retard.

Connor. But... ent it / betta if –

Birdie. Fuck no. No... definitely no.

Matty. Girls don't wanna know that shit bruv. You fink she'll bang ya, if you tell 'er?
Connor the mong, fuckin everyfink up again.

Birdie. Why d'ya fink you still ent lost it?

Connor. I dunno... I just –

Matty. Coz ya keep fuckin tellin' 'em. Fuckin girl's man, they want a lad wiv experience.
Ya do wanna finally get ya dick wet, ennit?

Conner. Yeah course I do.
She's really nice.
But I just don't wan –

Matty. She's never gonna open 'er legs bruv. No fuckin chance.

Birdie. Only if you tell 'er though.
Like, she might still give ya nosh. But she ent gonna fuck ya.

Matty. Best fing to do is act confident. Boss that shit. Don't fuckin flap it 'n shake like a little pussy.
Touch 'er up a bit first.
To Birdie. They fuckin love a bit a hand down there, ennit Birdie?

Birdie. Foe surrrrrre.

Matty and Birdie laugh together.

Matty. You gotta get 'er wet. Then when she's proppa moist, like fuckin drippin' just ask 'er for a fuck 'n slip it up 'er. That's what I'd do.

Connor. Really? Should I?

Birdie. Yes mate. Fuck sake. You gotta take control. If she ent onea them frigid bitches then she'll blatantly do anyfink if ya tell 'er to.

Matty. That's what they want.

Connor. I don't fink I can just start touchin' 'er up though.

Matty. Why?

Connor. Can't I just wait till –

Matty. What? Till ya fuckin eighty or sumink?

Connor. No. Just... like, just let it happen naturally?

Birdie. *Naturally?*

Matty. Don't be a fuckin pussy. If ya wanna be a virgin the rest of ya life then… yeah let it happen. *Naturally.*

Birdie. It's only fanny, Connor.

Connor. It's just… I really really like 'er. An' I don't want 'er laughin' at me cos I don't know what I'm doin'. She might tell me to do one 'n stuff.

Matty. Well don't tell 'er you're a fuckin virgin then. Prick.
An' I fort you'd be used to peeps creasin' at ya by now.
Hardly like you're the sharpest lad round town, is it?
Connor the fuckin mong.
What was that place you went to?
Some fuckin spazdic centre or sumink, weren't it?

Birdie. C'mon mate. Time to man up.

Matty. Tell ya what. I'll go round instead, yeah?
I'll sort 'er out good 'n proppa. She'll fuckin love it.
I'll feed 'er my massive fuck off *Godzilla* cock till the slag chokes.
I'll proppa destroy it.
Like, annihilate that shit.
Like, she'll 'av to fuckin claim disability benefits or sumink when I'm done minin' out that fanny of 'ers.
Why d'ya fink they call me the *Demolition Man*?

Connor. NO!
Please don't.

Don't say fings like that.
I really like 'er.

Matty. I'll say what the fuck I want, ya fuckin mong.
Tryin' to tell me 'n shit.

Birdie. He's only messin' Connor.
We wanna help you mate. We're gonna get your cherry popped tonight, I promise ya that.
You just gotta do as we say 'n you'll be sorted.

Connor. Yeah?

Ok.

Matty. *To Birdie.* I'm fuckin gaggin' for a bine.

Birdie. Same.
'Ow much money you got, Connor?
We only need like a bluey. Just enough for a pack like.

Connor. Err… Ok, fink I've got enough.

Birdie. Sound.

Connor. Can I 'av one of 'em?

Birdie. Course man.
We need 'em to skin up wiv when we get the spice though so only one, oright?

Connor. Yeah ok, Birdie.

Lights fade.

Five

Lina

Cradles her crying baby.

Hush, little baby, don't say a word.
Papa's gonna buy you a mockingbird

And if that mockingbird won't sing,
Papa's gonna buy you a diamond ring

And if that diamond ring turns brass,
Papa's gonna buy you a looking glass

And if that looking glass gets broke,
Papa's gonna buy you a billy goat –

The sound of a microwave ding.
Lina walks over to the microwave and takes out a bottle of milk – Baby stops crying.

How am I meant to be a mom?
When I can't even cope by myself
It's all the time
Twenty four fuckin seven
I need sleep

I need my space
I *need* silence
But she won't *stop* crying.
I feel so helpless
I can't stop her
I don't like it
It's like she's in pain all the time
All she does is cry
It hurts my head
My whole body hurts
I just want her to stop
No one told me it would be this hard

I googled baby support groups
But they're all so fuckin far away
I don't drive
And I can't get the bus with a baby and all this shit I have
to cart round
I can't deal with this shit
Why is life so *fuckin* hard?
Beat.
The thought of having her with me
Depending on me forever
It makes me feel physically sick
I just want some help
Anyone
But there's no one

I didn't like my midwife in hospital
The way she spoke to me
Talking to me like I knew nothing
It was like she was angry at me for having a baby

She hardly let me hold her
In the end I discharged myself
They said I needed to stay a little longer
Fuck that, I thought
I just couldn't hack being in there anymore

I was breastfeeding her
Only because they said it was better for them
But my nipples hurt so much
Like, tender to the touch
And it's been giving me these horrible cramps
Their like period pains but I'm not even on my fuckin
period
I hate it
So I've started using bottled milk
I hope it stops the pain
Beat.
The loneliness is creeping back
I can feel it irritating my bones
I thought having a kid would stop it
But it's even worse now
I feel more alone than ever
I regret everything
I regret moving to this shit town
I regret this shit flat
Beat.
I regret this fuckin kid
My daughter

Baby starts crying.
Lights fade.

Six

Lina's place – Connor and Lina sit close.

Lina. Why you so nervous?

Connor. Cos I –
I really like you.

Lina. Aw, that's cute.
But you don't need to be so nervous just because you like me.

Connor. Ok.

Lina. *Places her hand over his heart.* Flipin' ek, Connor. Your heart feels like it's gonna pop out your chest. Are you broken or something?

Connor. I don't fink so.
Sorry.
I'll try 'n stop it beatin' so much.

Lina. *Laughs.* You're funny.

Lina pulls Connor's top up.

Lina. Wow.
I can see it beating through your skin.
That's really freaky... but kinda cool as well.
It's like. It's like it's trying to break free.
I like it.

Connor. I like your eyes.

Lina. Aww, thanks. I like your eyes too.
They remind me of maltesers.
And I like your hands. There nice 'n big.

Connor. Ok.

Connor places a hand high on Lina's thigh and try's to move to her crotch.

Lina. Woah.
Wait. Wait. What you doing, Connor?

Connor. Ah, I – I – I'm so sorry... I – I didn't meant to upset ya.
Sorry. I'm really sorr –

Lina. It's ok, Connor. It's ok. No worries.
Let's just take it slow. Ok?

Connor. Ok.

Long pause.

Lina. Tell me something about yourself?

Connor. Err... I dunno.

Lina. Relax, Connor.

Connor. *Thinks hard.* I've got a CAT!

It's my neighbour's cat but they let me look after it, A
LOT!

Lina. Ok... That's cool.
But... What about you though?
I wanna know about you.

Connor. *Thinks hard.* Err... I don't know.
Beat.
When I was born my umbilical cord wrapped around my
neck 'n chocked me. My mum told me it starved my brain
of oxygen. Only for a moment but... That's why I'm a bit of
a mong now.

Lina. What?
NO CONNOR!
You're not a *mong*.

Connor. Only a bit.

Lina. No. Don't call yourself that.
Why would you say that?

Connor. Coz everyone else does.

Lina. Well you're not. So no more of that. Ok?

Connor. *Smiles.* Ok.

Why d'ya live by ya-self?
I don't know anyone our age who lives in their own flat.
It's really cool.

Lina. It's not. Trust me. None of this is cool.
Beat.

My little brother was killed about five... six... FUCK!
I can't even remember when... It's gotta be like six years ago now, I think.
Beat.

He was hit by a speeding car, right outside our house.
Beat.

I saw it happen from my window.
He was only playing on his scooter over the road. He was crossing to come back in the house. When, when some stupid *fuckin* bitch who was too busy looking down at her phone hit him.
Beat.

The force of the impact pushed his head through the windscreen.

Connor. Ah no. I'm really sorry. That's so bad.

Lina. It was a long time ago, so... fuck it. What can you do?
I know it sounds terrible but I don't really think about him anymore. Only on his birthday. But I even forgot that this year.
Beat.

It's just, so much has happened since, you know?
My dad was never the same after. He couldn't handle it, losing his little boy.
I got in from school one day 'n that was it. Gone. My mum told me he had just gone for a few day to get his head sorted 'n then he'd be back.
But five years on 'n I still haven't saw or heard from him.

He was a weak, weak man. He had no right to just go, you know?

What about me? I still needed him.

Connor. What 'bout your mum?

Lina. After dad left it was just me 'n her for a bit… And what a massive fuckin bitch she become.
Beat.
She kicked me out last year. That's why I moved here.

Connor. Why?

Lina. Why what?

Connor. Why she kick you out?

Lina. *Beat.*
I fucked her boyfriend.
The cow deserved it.
I don't know what it was with her… she would never…
AUGH!
Beat.
She never help me. With anything.
She never wanted me round her, you know? It was like I was fuckin invisible or something.

Connor. 'Ow could you be invisible to anyone? Even if I was blind I'd still remember your face it's that nice.

Lina. *Smiles.* That's really cute, Connor.

I don't think anyone's said anything like that to me before. Thanks.
Beat.
Shame my mum thought different.

Connor. Why?

Lina. Cos... Things only really got bad between us the past few years.
Beat.
She was jealous of me. It was plastered all over her battered old face.
Fuckin bitch got bitter when her little girl started to grow tits bigger than hers. An' as she got saggy 'n I developed 'n started getting the attention from the men she liked. She did the only thing she's ever known how to do well, and that's taking shit out on me.

Only reason she let me stay at the house so long was because she felt like she had some fuckin obligation because dad had gone.
So I just had to give her a good enough reason to kick me out.
Beat.
So I fucked her man.
He'd been wanting it ever since he moved in.
Looking me up 'n down whenever I walked in the room.
Gorping at my arse.
It got to the point where I deliberately started walking round in just a t-shirt. I wanted to get him going.
I enjoyed it. Knowing he was looking at me.

I only really liked it because I knew he liked me more than
her.
I wanted her to catch me fuckin him on *her* bed.
I just wanted her to feel something for me, you know?
Even if it was hate.
I just wanted a reaction.
Anything.

Connor. So what happened?

Lina. She slapped me about a bit.
Yanked on my hair.
Pushed me down the stairs.
An' kicked me out.
Beat.
I don't think she meant it, though.
The pushing me down the stairs, but you know. She might
as well of.

Connor. At least you got a reaction.

Lina. Yeah… At first it was worth it to see the reaction on
her face… but…
I don't know.
Fuck it.
What's done is done. Not like I can take it back, is it?
Beat.
I'm a massive fuck up.

Connor. NO! You're really. *Really* nice. No one's ever been
as nice to me as you.

Lina. I'm a dirty slag.

A fucking. Waste of space, bitch who needs to crawl under a rock and die.

Connor. NO! Don't say that, Lina.

Lina. Yeah, well. *Pause.* That's what my mum thinks, anyway.
Beat.
Everyone I've ever loved has gone, Connor.
They've either runaway.
Kicked me out or their dead.
Even the dad of my baby fucked off cos he couldn't handle me.
Like. I don't –

Baby starts crying.
Lina picks the baby up from the cot.

Lina. I'm really sorry.
She's always crying.

Connor. It's ok.
I love babies.

Lina. Hush, little baby, don't say a word.
Papa's gonna buy you a mockingbird

And if that mockingbird won't sing,
Papa's gonna buy you a diamond ring

Connor. My parents used to sing that to me.

Lina. Yeah mine too.
Well, my dad did anyway.

Some time passes. The baby is still crying.

Lina. Connor, she's not stopping.
Do you wanna hold her?

Connor. Yeah oright.

Lina gives the baby to Connor.
Connor begins to sing while he gently rocks the baby.

Connor. Hush, little baby, don't say a word.
Papa's gonna buy you a mockingbird —

Baby stops crying.

Lina. *Smiles.* She must like you.
Pause.
You're pretty good with kids, aren't you?
I like that.

Connor. *Whispers.* What's its name?

Lina. Hope.

Connor. That's so beautiful.
Is it a girl's name?

Lina. *Laughs.* Yes, Connor.

A loud knock at the door.
Baby starts crying.
Lights fade.

Seven

Lina's place – Lina, Connor, Birdie and Matty sit on sofas
drinking alcohol. Lina douse not look amused.

Matty. Nah man. Nah. You're all gettin' me wrong. I'm
not like that... but if I was, then why not?
You know what I'm sayin'?

Lina. Not really.

Birdie. Bruv, what the fuck?

Matty. I don't mean if you accidentally kill someone... or if
it's onea them... them, err... crimes of punishment fings or
sumink like that.

Lina. *Laughs.* Crimes of passion?

Matty. Ya what?

Lina. Don't you mean crimes of passion?

Matty. *Tuts.* Yeah, that's what I said.
Lina. No it wasn't. You said –

Matty. *Kisses his teeth.* Whatever man.

All I'm sayin' is, if you plan that shit 'n you get a buzz from it... Ahh... what's it called? Err... ya know?

Lina. Premeditated?

Matty. Yeah that's it... I fink.

You're gonna get collared for it, ennit? So why not? It's not like it's worse than killin' someone is it? So you'd 'av nufink to lose.

I'm just sayin', like. You're fucked anyway so If you're gonna kill someone then you might as well rape 'em too.

Lina. You'd fuck a corpse?

Matty. WHAT?

Fuck no bitch. Listen.

You'd do it before ya killed 'em, ennit?

Unless you're into bangin dead peeps 'n shit.

I'm just sayin', if all that psycho shit did float ya boat, then why not?

I don't get it when peeps say they wouldn't.

You's get me now, ennit?

Lina. Yeah, *obviously.*

Birdie. I know what ya sayin' Matty.

Matty. Yeah, whatever man. Fuck it.

Just sayin' that's all.

To Lina. Is that the new iphone?

Lina. Yeah.

Matty. Sick. Let us 'av a look?

Matty snatches the phone from the table before Lina has chance to react.
He briefly examines it then drops it in his drink.

Lina. WHAT THE FUCK!
You fuckin *twat*.
Why did you do that?

Matty. Oright, fuckin chill man. Sorry 'bout that. It slipped out me hand.

Lina. You. You're a fuckin twat.
Why did you do that?

Matty. It just slipped man. Oright. What the fuck?
Weren't even my fault. Soz, but ya know what iphones are like, ennit?

Lina tries to switch it on.

Lina. FUCKIN 'ELL. It's not working now.
I can't fuckin believe this.

Connor. Rice. Fink that works.

Birdie. Yeah yeah, rice. Put it in rice. That's the one man.

Lina. *To Birdie.* What you doing?
Birdie. What?

Lina. That. What is it?

Birdie. Just some spice. Chill.

Lina. You having a fuckin laugh?
You're not smoking that shit in here.

Birdie continues.
Baby starts crying.

Matty. Fuck this shit man.
Shut that fing up will ya?

Lina puts her baby in another room.
Muffled crying can still be heard.

Lina. Who are you two anyway?
Haven't you got anywhere better to be?

Birdie. Yeah man, Me n Matty are entrepreneur. We're goin' places.
We're gonna be like Scarface, rollin' round in ah gold-plated Lambo's, mansions, birds on either side of us, everyfink.
Ennit Matty?

Matty. Deffo bruv.

Connor. Thought you said we were equal partners?

Birdie. Ah yeah man, course we are buddy.
To Lina. Yeah man, the three of us are goin' places man.
Movin' up 'n shit. Gettin' outa this shit'ole for good.

Lina. Do you drive?

Birdie. Nah man.

Lina. Not gonna get that far then are ya boys?

Matty. *Tuts.* What you on 'bout. Ya takin' the piss or
sumink?

Lina. No. Just saying.

Matty. I can fuckin drive. Fuck a licence though. Costs doe
man.

Connor. I'm havin' lessons. I can drive for you's.

Lina. Connor, what you doing with these idiots?

Matty. Oi bitch. Watch ya mouth.

Lina. Yeah whatever.
I think it's time you all leave now anyway.

Lights fade

Eight

Lina's place.

Matty. 'Ow many lads you fucked then?

Lina. None of your fuckin business.

Matty. Ah c'mon. It's just an innocent question.

Birdie. Yeah c'mon. 'Ow many?

Lina. CONNOR! Are you just gonna –

Birdie. Don't look at him for help.
'Ow many?

Matty. Why you so fuckin bothered?
Birds normally can't wait to fuckin boast 'bout who they bang.

Lina. I don't know you.
I didn't even fuckin invite you round and you're asking me this shit.

Birdie. 'Ow many?

Connor. Guys, please don't.

Birdie. Shut up Connor.
To Lina. C'mon?

Lina. Fuckin 'ell.
I don't know… A few.

Birdie. *To Matty.* Blatantly bucket loads, ennit?

Matty. Yeah man. Hundreds bruv. Not includin' blowies though, obviously.

Birdie. She's probably got a bucket n'all.
To Lina. 'Ow many dicks you sucked?
No… 'Ow many you sucked, just this week?

Matty. She's got some fine blowjob lips.
To Lina. C'mon, 'Ow many ya noshed on this week?

Birdie. C'mon. Ya –

Lina. How many you two sucked?

Matty. *Tuts.* Shut up, bitch.
Fuckin slag, runnin' ya mouth 'n shit.

Lina. Or do you two just suck each other's?
Yeah that's it.

Birdie. Who d'ya think ya talkin' to? Ya fuckin sket.

Matty. You wanna watch ya mouth man.
You don't wanna know what we do to dutty sket's like you when the start runnin' their mouths.

Birdie. Ah, look. We're sorry. That was outa order. We were only messin' man.
We never meant to upset ya.

Friends?

Lina. Yeah you fuckin did. And... whatever. I need to clean up and stuff so can you all go now?

Birdie. Ah yeah man, course. Sorry 'bout all that man. Just...

I think... You should fuck Connor before we go.

Lina. What?

Matty. That was why you invited him round, ennit?

Lina. No. Course I fuckin didn't. I'm not fuckin anyone.

Connor. I'm sorry. I didn't mean for them to –

Lina. Can you all just leave now?

Please?

Birdie. Ah c'mon we're only messin'.

Matty. No were not.
Why won't you fuck 'im?
Like, I know he's a ginger cunt... And a bit of a mong, but still.

Lina. Just leave?

Connor. Lina –

Lina. You too Connor.
Leave now.

GET THE FUCK OUT!

I'm not joking.
You all need to go… or I'm calling the police.

Matty. Go on then.

Lina tries to use her phone but it's still not working.

Lina. Oh my God.
You fuckin planned this.

Birdie. We were just bored man, that's all. Fort we'd have
a bit a fun.
C'mon do him a favour.

Lina. *Beat.*

Ok.

Birdie / Matty. Ya what?

Birdie. You serious?

Lina. I'll fuck him. But not with you two watching.

Matty. You for real though?

Lina. Yeah.
If you all promise to fuck off after? Then... yeah I will.

Birdie. Hear that bruv. Buzzin' man. You're gettin' some fanny tonight.
I fuckin told ya.

Lina. Leave then.
I'll send him out after.

Birdie and Matty leave the room.

Lina. Go on then. Drop 'em.

Connor begins to undo his trousers.

Lina. Do you really want this Connor?
Am I that... special?

Connor. It's just... I need to tell you sumink.

Lina. What Connor?
What the fuck is this?
I thought it was just gonna be the two of us?
Who the fuck are they?

Connor. I – I need to tell you...

Lina. WHAT CONNOR?

Connor. Nothing.

Baby starts crying.
Lights fade.

<u>Nine</u>

Lina's place – Lina is behind a sofa, unseen by the
audience.

Matty. Go on then. This is what ya been waitin' for, ennit?

GO ON!

Connor. I can't.

Matty. Look at 'er. She's fuckin gaggin' for some cock.
Your cock. Or are ya some fuckin queere fuck?
Stop flappin' it ya fuckin gay boy.

Lina. Connor no.

Birdie. Shut the fuck up.
He ent gonna be long. HAAA!

Matty. Go on.

Birdie. GO ON CONNOR! What you fuckin waitin' for
man? Smash that shit. She ent goin' nowhere.

Lina. NO!
You fuckin dare Connor.

Connor. *To birdie.* No.
I don't fink... This ent right.

Matty. What you on bruv?
She was the one who invited ya round.
Look at 'er. She got all nice 'n dressed up for ya 'n everyfink.

Holds Connors head forcing him to look at Lina.

Look at 'er.
All that makeup plastered over that pukka face.
She did all this for you.
And 'er hair.
That's fancy, ennit?
LOOK AT HER, YA FUCKIN PRICK!

Birdie. Now's ya time to man up. Whip it out 'n bang it.
End of.
We ent doin' this for no fuckin reason.
You know that, ennit Connor?

Matty. If you don't fuck 'er I will.

Connor. NO!
Pleassse just stop.

Sobs. I just wanna go home.
My mum's gonna be wonderin' where I am.

Birdie. *To Matty.* Meh meh meh. The mong wants to go home. HAA!

Matty. You ent goin' nowhere till you pop ya cherry, oright.
We're doin' this for you bruv.
We're finally gettin' you some fanny.
You should be fankin' us. Not flappin' it like a little bitch.

Birdie. C'mon, just get on wiv it man.
Not like you's two are gonna go skippin' off down the street together now is it? Just fuckin do it and let's go.
We've gotta get back to earnin.

Matty. Connor, Last chance or she's mine and you can watch.

Connor. OK!
Ok.

Connor moves in.

Lina. CONNOR!
NO PLEASE CONNOR!

NO!

Matty. Fuck this shit. If that little pricks gettin' some then I want some n'all.
Got me all fuckin goin' 'n shit.

Birdie. Fuck that man. We'll be time Matty. Just leave it man.

Matty. Nah bruv. I'm fuckin gaggin' for a bit a pussy. You sin that tight arse on 'er? She's got a proppa bangin' body.

Birdie. Matty… what 'bout sloppy seconds?
Fuck that.

Matty. Fuck it. I'll go up 'er dirt track instead. Ha ha.

Birdie. Whatever man. Just make it quick. Fuck sake.

Baby starts crying.
Lights fade.

Ten

Lina's place.
Sound of the baby crying – It builds in volume.
Lina is alone, Connor, Birdie and Matty have left
Lina is curled up on the floor weeping.
She covers her ears to try and drown out the sound.

Crying gets louder.

Lina gets up.
She picks up her baby and cradles it in her arms.

Lina. Hush, little baby, don't say a word —
Papa's —
Papa's gonna buy you a mockingbird —

And —

Crying becomes louder.

Lina. And if that mockingbird won't sing,
Papa's gonna buy you a — diamond —

And if that diamond ring turns —

Baby still crying.

*Lina completely covers the baby by wrapping it in a
blanket.*
*She walks over to the microwave and places her baby
inside.*

Crying can still be heard.

Lina is still weeping.
She turns on the microwave.
*She goes back to the middle of the room and curls up on
the floor.*
She places her hands over her ears.

Beat.

Baby stops crying.
Sound of Lina weeping.
Lights fade.

End of play

Hush Little Baby was inspired by true events

Case one In 2011 China Arnold was convicted for the murder of her 28 day old daughter after she put her in a microwave oven for two minutes following an argument with the father over the baby's paternity.

Case two In 2015 Ka Yang was convicted for the murder of her seven week old daughter after she put her in a microwave oven for over five minutes because she was being – Quote 'Irritable and fussy and holding her back from work'.

For inquiries email phillipdarkins@gmail.com

Printed in Great Britain
by Amazon

69240662R00051